BRIC LUCY

Wants
a Pet

BRIGID LUCY

wants a Pet

Leonie Norrington

Illustrated by Tamsin Ainslie

LITTLE HARE

www.littleharebooks.com

Text copyright © Leonie Norrington 2011

Illustrations copyright © Tamsin Ainslie 2011

First published 2011

National Library of Australia
Cataloguing-in-Publication entry

Norrington, Leonie.
Brigid Lucy wants a pet / by Leonie Norrington ;
illustrated by Tamsin Ainslie.
1st ed.
978 1 921541 69 8 (pbk.)
Norrington, Leonie. Brigid Lucy ; 1.
Pets—Juvenile fiction.
Animals, Mythical—Juvenile fiction.
Ainslie, Tamsin, 1974-
A823.3

Cover design by Vida & Luke Kelly
Set in 13/19 pt Stone Informal by Clinton Ellicott
Printed by WKT Company Limited
Printed in Shenzhen, Guangdong Province, China, December 2010

5 4 3 2 1

This product conforms to CPSIA 2008

Contents

For my firstborn granddaughter,
Bethany Lorraine Norrington—LN

For Melissa Mackie—TA

Prologue

Hello. Who are you?

A reader!

How **exciting**, because I'm a writer. Well, a storyteller-writer-kind-of-person-thing. I tell all the stories about me and my best friend, Biddy.

But don't ask me what I look like. I don't show up in the mirror, and Biddy can't tell me, because she can't see me.

But I reckon I might look like this . . .

Or this . . .

Or even this . . .

I definitely don't look
like that . . .

Or that . . .

Yucki-toenails! I would never want
to have pointy ears or long feet.

Where did I come from?

Well, me and Biddy used to live in
the country. Biddy and her family lived
on her grandfather's farm, and I lived
nearby in the **Great Bushland**. But
then her dad got a new job and we had to
move to the city.

How did we meet?

Well, you see, one day, I was all by

myself, sitting on some jewel-beetle casing, and tobogganing down the smooth bark of a white gum tree. It was fun. But I had already done it nine thousand and forty-two times. **Shooh!**

I was flying down once again when I heard a loud sob. It gave me such a fright, I forgot to stop and, **zuuup!** I flew through the air. And, **plonk!** I landed in a tangle of little-human-girl's hair. It was soft and cuddly and wet with tears.

The owner of the hair was sitting under the gum tree, and cuddling two huge drippy-tongue dogs. 'I'm not leaving my friends,' the little girl said. 'I'm not going to the city.'

'Friends?' I said, quickly disentangling myself from her hair. 'Have you got friends? I've been living in this Great Bushland for nine thousand, four hundred and sixty-two years. I have always wanted a friend.'

But the girl ignored me. She kept on

3

sobbing and saying things to the dogs, like, 'I'm staying right here with you, Pocket and Lacey.' And, 'I don't care if I starve to death and **die**.'

I quickly ran out onto the girl's nose.

'Excuse me,' I yelled, waving my arms. 'Dogs are not friends. They are pets. But, I could be your friend. Please, please, please. Can I be your friend?'

But she didn't answer me. That's when I realised that she couldn't see me or hear me, so I just stayed in her hair and became her bestest friend in the whole world all by myself.

And it has been so exciting! We've been on a plane and in cars and in trains. We've seen millions of different kinds of people.

Don't I miss my home?

No. I totally love the city. But Biddy **hates** it.

Biddy had lots of pets on the farm. She had a pony, six sheep, and two dogs. She also had rabbits that disappeared and reappeared like magic in the back paddock, and chooks that laid golden-brown eggs.

But Biddy's not allowed to have pets in the city because her mum says 'the-garden-is-too-small' and 'it-would-be-cruel' to have a pony, or a drippy-tongue dog in such a tiny garden. Biddy wants a cat but I hate cats to impossibility. They catch all sorts of tiny creatures!

Anyway we don't need a cat. Why can't we have the grasshoppers and snails and **beetles** that already live in the garden? Or slugs! They're cute and they leave magical silvery tracks behind themselves that sparkle in the moonlight.

So, that's the problem. (You know how all stories have to have a problem? Well that is the problem for this story.) Biddy wants a nasty old cat and I don't. And now I'm going to tell you the story . . .

Oh. Wait a minute—I have to start it properly . . .

'Long, long ago . . .'

No, I can't say that because it is
happening right now . . .

'Once upon a time . . .'

'No! Stop, Daddy! No!' Biddy is yelling.
And she's running.

Hang on! I'm slipping. We are
getting into the story already. I have to
grab Biddy's hair to stop from falling off
her head.

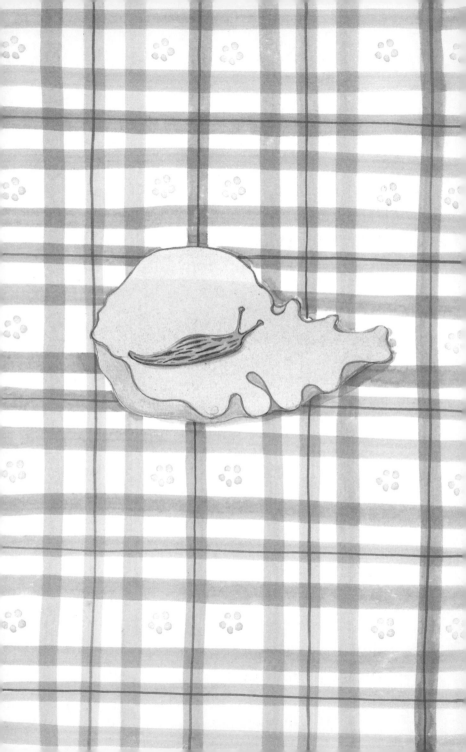

Chapter one
a special pet

'Daddy, stop!' calls Biddy, as she flies into the kitchen, with me bouncing at the end of a strand of her hair. 'Don't eat Oscar!' she says.

Biddy's dad is standing at the kitchen bench, his mouth open. He's holding a piece of lettuce, ready to bite. He stops. 'Who's Oscar?' he says.

'My pet slug,' Biddy says, pointing to the lettuce leaf.

Biddy's dad looks at the lettuce leaf and sees the slug. '**Ahhh!**' he screams and flings the piece of lettuce across the floor. Biddy's dad is not very brave.

Biddy runs to pick up the lettuce leaf. 'Oscar! Are you all right?' she says.

'What's all this noise about?' Mum asks. She climbs over the baby rail that keeps Biddy's little sisters (Miss Getting-All-The-Attention Matilda and Crybaby Ellen), away from the dangerous knives and hot-breath stoves in the kitchen.

Dad and Biddy spin around together.

'Brigid put a slug in the salad,' Dad yells.

'Daddy tried to eat Oscar,' Biddy yells even louder.

'Stop!' Mum puts her hands up for silence. 'Brigid Lucy, did you put a slug in our salad?' she asks.

'I was going to take him out before we ate it,' Biddy tells her.

'I nearly ate a slug,' Dad says. His face is going green.

'Anyway, Dad,' Biddy says, hands on hips, 'Mum said we're not allowed to take food from the bowl before dinner. She said we have to wait till it's on the table. So you were being naughty.'

'I beg your pardon?' says Biddy's dad.

His eyes go big and his face goes red.
I block my ears before he yells, 'Brigid Lucy.
Go to your room!'

Which is **totally** unfair. He's the one
that pinched the lettuce.

So, as Biddy storms off down the hall to
her bedroom, I yell, 'Fine then! Next time
we won't save you from eating a slug.'

But, of course, he can't hear me, so he
doesn't listen.

Now here we are, me and Biddy, sitting on
Biddy's bed. Biddy doesn't care about being
sent to her room. She just sits, sucking her
thumb, till someone comes to let her out.

But I **hate** being sent to Biddy's room.
And I hate it even worse when Biddy sucks
her thumb, because it's as if her thumb is
her best friend instead of me.

I don't like Oscar the slug much right
now, either. He doesn't even care that
Biddy's in trouble and it's all his fault.

He just keeps eating, munch, munch, munch on his silly piece of lettuce.

Finally, after days and days (or a long time anyway), Dad's footsteps come down the hall. Biddy quickly pulls her thumb out of her mouth. She hides its wetness under her pillow, before Dad can tell her off about being too-old-to-suck-her-thumb.

'Brigid,' Dad says, sitting down next to her on the bed. 'Why . . .?'

Biddy's dad is not very good at telling people off. He only knows how to yell, and how to go to work, and how to fix broken toys, and stuff like that.

He stays quiet for a minute. Then he tries to tell Biddy off again. 'A slug?' he says, but he doesn't know what else to say.

Biddy knows it is going to take ages for Dad to tell her off and let us out of her room, so she tries to help him. 'I only put Oscar in the lettuce because he was hungry,' she says. 'You have to feed pets every day.'

'A pet?' Dad says. 'You can't have a slug for a pet.'

'That's the only pet I can have,' Biddy cries, 'because the garden is too small for a pony or a dog, and my dad won't let me have a cat.' Tears sparkle in her eyes.

'Biddy,' Dad says, as he puts his arm around her, 'I'm allergic to cats.'

'Well, you shouldn't eat **junk food**,' says Biddy.

'Allergies don't come from junk food,' Dad says.

'They do so!' Biddy cries. 'Mum said they do. That's why we're not allowed to have lollies and preservatives.' And thinking about not having lollies makes Biddy so sad, she starts to cry really loudly.

So loudly that Mum comes in with Biddy's baby sister, Ellen, on her hip.

Hearing Biddy cry makes Ellen start to cry, too.

'Biddy, darling,' Mum says. '**Shhh, shhh!**' She squashes Biddy and Ellen up together in a hug.

Mum glares at Dad with a see-what-you've-done look on her face. Then she says to Biddy, 'It's okay, darling. Mummy's here now.' And, 'That's-enough-crying.' And, 'Take-Oscar-outside-to-eat-some-grass.'

'He-he-he doesn't like gr-gr-grass,' Biddy hiccups. 'He o-o-o-nly likes lettuce.'

'He will like grass,' Mum says, helping Biddy up off the bed and out of the door. 'Just take him outside and let him try it. I'm sure he'll love it.'

'**Yippee!** We're getting out of the bedroom!' I yell, doing cartwheels across the top of Biddy's head.

Chapter two
a backyard adventure

Before we moved to the city, me and Biddy used to have the best fun in the backyard on the farm. We would throw sticks for the dogs, and find mice in the shed and toads under the rocks, and catch worms and beetles. We'd hunt for unicorns and fillikizard dragons that can kill you dead with one **whooh!** of their stinky breaths.

If we found a toadstool ring, we made up stories about the fairies who would come and dance there. (We learnt all about fairies in Biddy's fairy books. They are little magical creatures that act exactly like the shadowy, cheeky yebil yebils, and the big-eyed, hairy choolkas that live in the Great Bushland, where I come from.

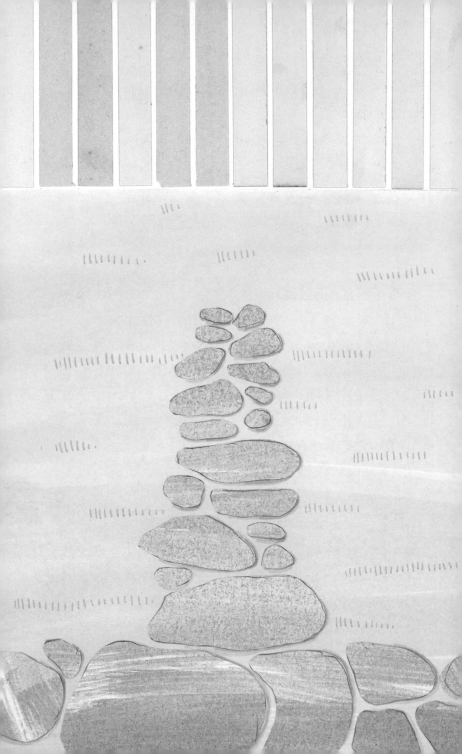

But the fairies look totally different.)

I love the city, but me and Biddy can't have adventures in this city backyard. It is so little, we can see the whole garden with just one looking. And there's a fence that runs all the way around it, so a fillikizard dragon or a unicorn couldn't get in, even if it wanted to.

And Biddy is not allowed to climb the fence. Not even to see if Jamie, our next-door neighbour, is home. Mum says this is because Biddy might fall-off-the-fence-and-break-her-leg. And there are no trees to climb. There is just a crinkly green lawn that is squashed as flat as concrete.

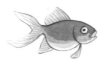

Biddy sits down near the fence, where the lawn is a bit longer, and puts Oscar down to eat some grass. Before Biddy got in trouble, I thought Oscar was a good pet. But now I think he is boring.

All he wants to do is eat. So, I don't want to look after Oscar. I want to play imagination.

Biddy wants to play imagination, too. 'This is a **fairy** ring,' she says. She picks up lengths of dried grass and makes them into a circle. 'Tonight the fairies will come and dance under the full moon.'

I pretend to be a fairy, and grab some dried grass to make a brightly coloured scarf. Then I twirl the scarf around my head as Biddy tells her story.

'And glow-worms blink like party lights around the circle,' she says. 'And the full moon hangs above them like a great disc of solid silver.' Then she lowers her voice, and narrows her eyes to make them look mystical. 'The fairies dance and sing so loudly, they can't hear the soft flicker of leather wings, or the **crunch** of great, curved claws in the darkness, sneaking closer and closer,' Biddy continues.

Suddenly, there *is* a flicker of wings.

A magpie lands on the fence beside us. He lifts his head up and starts to sing. His song trills and warbles all around us. Then he swoops down and lands beside us. Biddy stays perfectly still, not even blinking her eyes. She's pretending to be a towel, fallen from the washing line, because the magpie would never come so close if he knew she was human.

He hops closer and closer.

But he's not looking at us. What's he looking at?

Oscar?

OSCAR!

A dive, a flap of wings, and the magpie is back on the fence, with Oscar in his beak. **Shake, whack, gulp!** Oscar's gone!

'You big fat meanie!' Biddy screams, running towards the magpie.

The magpie flies off the fence and flaps away.

Biddy flops down onto the grass, sobbing.

'What's wrong?' Mum and Dad call. They come running out of the house. 'Biddy, are you okay?' they say.

'A magpie ate Oscar,' Biddy wails.

Dad crouches down. 'Poor Biddy,' he says, as he puts his arm around her.

Mum says, 'I think we'll have to get Biddy a proper pet.'

'Really?' Biddy says. She stops crying. 'Can I choose it myself?'

'Yes,' Dad smiles. 'You most certainly can.'

'**No!**' I yell at them. 'She will choose a cat! I'll get eaten to death or have to escape and live all by myself, alone, like a no-best-friend person again.'

I run right to the top of Biddy's hair to yell louder at Biddy's dad. 'You can't let her have a cat. Aren't you allergic to cats?'

But of course he doesn't hear me, so he doesn't answer. Oh, it's just no use. I flop down to sulk. I bet he was just pretending to be allergic to cats. Grown-ups are the biggest fibbers sometimes.

Chapter three
a most exciting present

The next day, when Dad comes home
from work, he calls, 'Brigid Lucy?' as he
walks through the door. He has a 'surprise-
present' smile on his face and a box in his
hands.

Uh-oh! There could be a cat in that box,
I think. *What am I going to do?*

'Thank you! **Thank you!**' Biddy says.
She runs to take the present box and then
sits on the kitchen floor to open it.

I cross my fingers and my arms and my
legs and my eyes for luck. *Please not a cat.*
Please not a cat.

Biddy's little sister, Matilda, runs over,
too, and flops down to help Biddy open
the box.

'No, darling,' Mum says, as she comes into the kitchen, carrying little baby Ellen. She moves Ellen to her other hip and lifts Matilda up.

'No, leeb me!' Matilda cries, and struggles to get down. This makes Ellen start to cry, so Mum has to put Matilda down.

'Biddy, open the box at the table,' Mum says, 'so Matilda can't touch it.'

Biddy stands up and smiles nicely at Matilda. 'No, Matilda,' she says, holding the box high, like a big girl. 'You are too small for this present.'

Biddy carries the box over to the kitchen table. Then she undoes the ribbon, unwraps the paper and, finally, opens the box to look at the present.

Inside is a glass ball.

'It's a crystal ball,' Biddy says. 'A magic crystal ball.'

So it is! I think. **Wow!** We will be able to see what our next-door neighbour, Jamie, is doing in his room when he won't let us in.

How exciting! I love getting a crystal ball for a present!

Dad laughs. 'Biddy,' he says, 'it's not a crystal ball. It's a goldfish bowl.'

A goldfish bowl? I think. I'm disappointed.

'**Oh!**' Biddy says. She's disappointed, too. But then she realises that a fish is a pet. 'A goldfish!' she laughs. 'A pet goldfish. But where is he?'

'We'll get him on Saturday,' Dad tells her. 'You can choose him for yourself.'

I'm thinking, *A goldfish. Well, that* is *better than a horrible little-creature-catching cat. I could ride on a fish like the slivigools do.*

(Slivigools are beautiful magical creatures who live among the waving roots in the ponds in the Great Bushland. They love to ride fish.)

Yes, I think. *I might like a goldfish-kind-of pet.*

And Biddy thinks the same thing, too.

'Oh, Daddy, I love you to infinity!' she yells, cuddling him around the neck.

This makes Dad blush, and Mum smile, and Matilda **laugh**. Even baby Ellen is bouncing up and down on Mum's lap, smiling and clapping her hands.

Dad and Biddy fill the goldfish bowl with water and put it up on the kitchen bench, where Matilda can't reach it. Then they put in special blue pebbles, a plastic underwater castle, a small plant with tiny silver balls of air on its leaves, and a little shell that spits out bubbles.

I like this goldfish bowl. It sparkles, like the water where the slivigools sing, play, and swirl their long hair.

(Except the slivigool creeks have trees and birds nearby, and the creek water sings **tinkle-tinkle!** over the rocks and tree roots. So the goldfish bowl is a bit different.)

Then, on Saturday morning, Dad takes me and Biddy to buy a goldfish. Me and Biddy see the pet shop first. We can tell which one it is straightaway because through the window we can see cages and animals, and people pointing and choosing pets.

As Dad opens the shop door, he says, 'Brigid Lucy. Stay right beside me.' Then he holds his breath so he doesn't get allergic, and rushes inside the shop, past all the cages, to the fish tanks.

Me and Biddy do try to follow him. We really do. But the shop is absolutely brimming full with all kinds of pet animals. There are rabbits, and guinea pigs, and mice, and birds, and . . .

'Kittens!' Biddy yells.

'**Ahhh!**' I scream, and hide behind her ear. There is a glass cage full of baby cats. And no lid! What if they climb out?

'Daddy! Daddy! Please can we have a kitten?' Biddy calls. 'They're not *cats*, they're just little kittens. They wouldn't hurt anyone.' She leans into the cage and picks up one of the kittens.

I dive deep into one of Biddy's plaits. Not that I'm a scaredy chicken-heart or anything. But cats really are the most deadly **dangerous** of creatures.

'Don't play with the animals!' the pet-shop-owner lady snaps, and points to a sign on the wall. 'Can't you read?' She snatches the kitten from Biddy and drops it back into its cage.

Whew!

All the other people in the pet shop stare at Biddy. Biddy turns away from them and sees the birdcages. 'Dad! Look at the birds!' she calls.

I peek out of Biddy's hair. In the birdcages there are budgies, and parakeets, and quails, and tiny little finches, and a huge big parrot.

I climb out of Biddy's hair and sit on top of her head. 'Yes, Biddy, let's get a parrot!' I say.

'A parrot,' Biddy yells. 'Daddy, I could have a parrot!'

Dad is standing by the fish tanks calling, 'Biddy.'

But it's hard for me and Biddy to hear him while we are staring at the parrot.

So Dad calls a bit louder, 'Brigid!'

And then louder, 'Brigid, come here please, darling.'

And then, 'Brigid Lucy! Come here NOW!'

Biddy finally hears him and runs up to cuddle him. 'Daddy, this is the best place in the whole entire universe,' she says. 'Thank you for bringing me here!'

'Brigid, you have to concentrate,' Dad says. 'We have to choose a *f-f-ah*——' he says, lifting his head. 'Ah-CHOOO!' he sneezes, and then tries again.

'We have to choose a goldfish,' Dad says quickly, before the next sneeze comes. 'Ah-ah-ah-AH-CHOOO!'

Chapter four

a minor cat-astro-flee

Biddy tries to concentrate. Even though we both want to go back and look at the parrot. She makes herself look through the glass wall of the tank at the goldfish. The fish are all **floppy** tails and wobbly bodies and big wide eyes and gulpy-gulp mouths.

'I'd like that one,' she says. Then she changes her mind. 'No, no. I think I'd like that one, please.'

Dad signals to the pet shop lady to come over and catch the fish. '**Ah-CHOOO!**' he sneezes again, nearly blowing his handkerchief out of his hand. 'Show the lady which one, Biddy,' he says. 'Quickly! **Ah-ah-ah-ah-CHOOO!**'

But the more Biddy looks at the goldfish, the harder it is for her to choose.

First, she likes the one with the black spot.

But then, the big floppy one seems so nice and kind.

And, if she doesn't choose the sad-looking one, will anyone ever want him?

'Come on, Biddy. Let's go and see the birds,' I yell. But, of course, she doesn't hear me.

'What about the little **skinny** one?' Biddy says.

'I have other customers to attend to,'
the pet-shop lady tells Dad. 'These fish are
all exactly the same size. There is no reason
to choose.'

But Dad doesn't answer her, because
his eyes are full of tears, and his head is
tipping back, and he is sneezing. 'Ah-ah-
ah-ah-CHOOO!'

'Which ones are the girls?' Biddy asks
the pet-shop lady. And, 'But if I take just
one, will he get lonely all by himself?'

And, 'Is the one with the black spot friends with the one with the floppy tail?'

'You will take the one I catch for you,' the pet-shop lady snaps. She dips her net into the tank and scoops out just any old goldfish.

As soon as the lady scoops up the goldfish, me and Biddy **run** back to look at the parrot again. Imagine if Biddy could take him home for a pet! I could ride around on him like the tiny, magical creatures called ympes do.

(Ympes can actually attach themselves onto a bird's wings and fly with them right over the oceans to Alaska and Antarctica, where the whole world is white and blue.)

I'd love to take a ride on this parrot. But I've never flown on a bird before because it is dangerous. What if the parrot went right up into the sky and I fell off?

Or what if the parrot flew away and I never saw Biddy again? I'd be an all-by-myself, alone, no-best-friend person.

Oh look! Biddy wants me to fly. She's trying to open the birdcage for me. I should try flying in here, because the parrot can only fly around the shop. He can't get outside to fly too high, away to Alaska.

But the cage door is locked! The lock doesn't have a key.

Maybe it opens when someone says a magical unlocking-spell word, I think.

'**Oo-pen-doe-nous!**' I say. Nothing happens.

'**Till-gäng-lig!**' I say. Nothing happens again.

Perhaps it's not a magic-word lock. Maybe it works by magic control, like those remote boxes with buttons on them that you use to turn off a TV without even touching it.

I look around, and **yes!** There is a magic remote control on top of the parrot cage.

'Biddy! Biddy!' I yell.

Biddy spots the remote control at the same time I do. She picks it up, presses a button, and **click!** the birdcage opens.

'Thank you, Biddy,' I say. 'I'm going for a ride, but I won't be long.'

I jump off her shoulder, and scramble into the birdcage. Then I run up to the parrot and ask him if he will please take me for a ride.

I climb up on his back, hold on tight, and . . .

I'm flying! Flying through the cage door, and out into the shop. Flying around and around, right up high near the ceiling. I'm not even a bit scared.

I can see everything. There's the horrid pet-shop lady handing Dad the goldfish in a plastic bag.

'**Ah-CHOOO!**' he says, to thank her.

The other birds are flying with us. We're swooping and diving and screeching and squawking. The magic unlocking-remote unlocked *all* the cages in the shop.

There are lizards, and mice, and rabbits, and guinea pigs running all over the floor.

'Biddy, look at me!' I yell.

But Biddy doesn't. She is too busy looking at all the escaped animals. The pet-shop lady rushes to close the door and stop the animals from getting out.

A bald man climbs up on the shop counter, holding his hat against his chest.

A skinny lady hides by the birdcage, with her hands over her eyes.

'Get away from me,' a tall lady yells, with her back against the wall. She's pointing her umbrella like a sword at a big fat rat. 'Or I'll cut you to pieces.'

Biddy is running with delight from one animal to the next, scooping up one creature and talking to it, before putting it down again and picking up another one. She's forgotten all about me.

'*Biddy!* Biddy, come back!' I yell.

Chapter five

a goldfish-kind-of pet

'Calm down!' the pet-shop lady screams to her customers from the front of the shop. She spreads her arms and legs across the doorway, to stop them leaving.

But the customers are **scared** of the flapping birds and free animals, so they don't listen to the pet-shop lady. They just push straight past her. The parrot is heading for the door, too. What if he gets out after all, and flies away to Antarctica! I'd never see Biddy again!

I don't like flying any more. I want to go back to Biddy. But I can't, because now she's holding a ferret! A horrible ferret with **razor-sharp** teeth and evil, pointed claws. She doesn't even care about me being stuck on an escaping parrot.

'What if I fall off and hurt myself?' I yell to Biddy.

Then the pet-shop lady yells at Biddy as well. 'Put those animals down,' she barks. 'Where is your father?'

Dad is leaning against the wall near the goldfish tanks. His eyes are still watering, and he is still sneezing and sneezing.

'Kindly tell your child to put down my animals and leave!' the pet-shop lady snarls at Dad.

Biddy tells the ferret, 'Don't worry, I'll come back and visit.' But when she tries to put him down, he doesn't want to go back in the cage. He runs straight up to the top of Biddy's head instead.

'Don't be scared. It's all right,' Biddy says, in a kind voice. She carefully undoes his claws out of her scalp. But she takes so long that the pet-shop lady storms over, grabs the ferret from Biddy's head, and drops it back into its cage.

'Get out, the two of you!' the pet-shop lady orders Dad and Biddy, as she pushes them towards the door.

I ask the parrot, 'Please can you quickly drop me back to my friend?'

He swoops down and lands on Biddy's shoulder.

Biddy giggles, and stands perfectly still, her eyes wide with excitement.

'Thank you, thank you,' I tell the parrot, as I slip down through the softness of his feathers, into Biddy's hair. **Whew!** Home safe.

'Out! Out!' the pet-shop lady bellows.

Dad sneezes and tries to get his wallet out to pay the pet-shop lady for the goldfish.

'Don't worry,' she says. 'Just go.' She glares at Biddy like it was all her fault that the animals got free. Which it totally was not! It was the pet-shop lady's own fault. She should have put the magic remote up high out-of-the-reach-of-little-fingers.

That's what Biddy's mum said once to Dad when me and Biddy found his toolbox full of pointy nails and sharp saws.

When we get home, I fluff and wiggle to make a nest at the back of Biddy's hair and curl up.

I rode a parrot! I think. *A real-life parrot!* I close my eyes and remember the wind in my hair, and the thrill of being up so high. It was so much **fun**. I don't even care that Biddy nearly left me behind all by myself, because now we are back together, best friends again.

'I patted a kitten, and a guinea pig, and a ferret,' Biddy says, telling Mum all the pet-shop stories. 'And a parrot landed on my shoulder! *And* we didn't even have to pay for the goldfish!' she adds.

Mum says, 'Oh.' And, 'Fantastic.' And, 'Really!' She gets out her special POISON—DON'T TOUCH medicine box.

Then she looks inside to find Dad 'something-for-his-sneezing'.

After that, Mum helps Dad lie down on the couch with a special tablet and a special-smelling-kind-of bag, and tells him to close his eyes and rest.

Matilda wants to play with the goldfish.

'No, Matilda,' Biddy tells her, 'the germs on little kids' fingers make goldfish come up in lumps and boils, and they get bigger and bigger, till they **explode** into millions of——'

'Brigid!' Mum says, frowning. The frown is telling Biddy not to tell fibs.

'It's true, Mum,' Biddy says. Her eyes are wide with pretend innocence. 'The lady in the pet shop said so.'

'Brigid Lucy, stop telling stories right now,' says Mum.

Biddy sighs and turns to Matilda with a kind expression on her face. 'Matilda, **please** don't touch the goldfish,' she says.

Matilda says, 'Okay, Biddy.' She is being

good. She leans on the kitchen bench, her hands beneath her chin, and watches the goldfish go **gulp, gulp, gulp** inside the bubble of his plastic bag.

When Dad is feeling better, he shows Biddy how to put the goldfish in the bowl. I come out of Biddy's hair to help.

Dad places the plastic bag with the goldfish into the water in the goldfish bowl. He waits till the water inside the bag is exactly the same temperature as the water in the bowl. Then he lets the goldfish out of the bag to swim around. The goldfish's mouth opens and closes, opens and closes. Its eyes are big and wide. This goldfish is much more interesting than Oscar the slug.

'I'm going to call you **Rolly Polly**,' Biddy says to the fish.

Perhaps having a goldfish for a pet will be all right after all.

Chapter six
the book prize

I try to like Rolly Polly. I really do. It's just
that, from the top of the water, he looks
like a small wobbly gulp-gulp goldfish,
and from the side of the water he looks
like a big fat wobbly gulp-gulp goldfish.
And he doesn't do anything, except wiggle
and flap, **waggle** and float all day
long. Just like a no-brain greedy-pants
goldfish, covered in wobbly, floppy, flippy
bits of stuff. He doesn't even close his
eyes or blink.

And life is so totally boring with a
goldfish in the house. All Biddy does
for weeks and weeks is sit and talk to
the flobbidy old goldfish. Or is it days
and days?

Anyway . . . for the **whole** weekend—all Saturday afternoon and Sunday—all Biddy does is sit and talk to the goldfish. We have no fun at all. No playing imagination. No going to visit our next-door neighbour, Jamie. Nothing. I am desperate to do something exciting. I wish, wish, wish Biddy could see how boring that goldfish is.

On Monday morning, we are supposed to be packing our school lunchboxes and getting yelled at to 'hurry-hurry-and-get-ready-for-school' by Mum. But Biddy gets ready quickly and goes and sits at the kitchen bench, watching the goldfish.

Boring, boring, boring.

'. . . bored.'

Did Biddy just say *bored*? She did!

'Poor Rolly Polly,' she says. 'Are you bored?'

'Yes, he is,' I yell, jumping up and down on her arm. 'He is **totally** boring. Let's go and play something exciting.'

But Biddy just ignores me. 'Or are you depressed?' she says to the fish.

(Depressed is an important TV-word that means someone is sad and they need you to 'help them' and 'encourage them'.)

'No!' I yell. 'He's not depressed. He's just stupid and boring.'

But does Biddy listen to me? No!

'I would be depressed, too, if I had nothing exciting to do,' she says to Rolly Polly.

Then she jumps up. 'I know! I'll teach you to stand on your tail like a dolphin,' she says. 'If you were a tricky-dolphin goldfish, you would feel all **special** and not a bit sad.'

Tricks! I think. *That might be fun.*

'Watch me,' Biddy says, and does a handstand. 'See!' she says, in a funny upside-down voice.

She looks sideways to make sure that Rolly Polly is watching her. That makes her lose her balance. **Kick!** She hits the fruit bowl. It falls. **Crash!** And the noise gives her such a fright that, **whoops!** She tips sideways. **Whack!** She slams against the pot stand. **Clang, clang, clang!**

Pots scatter everywhere all over the floor.

'Biddy, what are you doing?' Mum yells from down the hall.

Biddy quickly gathers up all the pots and the fruit. 'Don't worry, handstands are easier in water,' she says to Rolly Polly. 'You'll be okay. Just have a try.'

But Rolly Polly doesn't have a try. He just keeps going around the bowl, **gulp-gulp-gulping**, like a totally dumb, floppy, can't-even-blink goldfish.

'Brigid Lucy,' Mum calls as she comes into the kitchen, 'are you ready for school?'

And then we have to get in the car and go to school.

Yes! I love school.

School is so exciting! Today is Assembly Day. This is the day the teachers give out prizes to the best kids. Miss Hopeful, Biddy's teacher, said that someone in Biddy's class was going to get a prize.

The prize is for being the best behaved.
And, it is a book voucher. Me and
Biddy love books. And Biddy has been
absolutely the best behaved since
Miss Hopeful told us about the prize.
So Biddy knows she is going to win. She
even knows what she's going to buy with
the book voucher. *An Encyclopedia of
Magical Creatures.*

We're sitting up the front of the school
hall. The teachers are sitting on the stage.
The boy or girl who gets the prize has to
walk up in front of everyone and say thank
you and smile, like a really special
person. Biddy is sitting up really straight
with her legs crossed and her eyes-to-the-
front-ears-listening-hard. And I'm sitting
right on top of her head so I can see
everything.

Miss Hopeful walks to the microphone
and starts to speak. 'And the prize for being
the best behaved goes to . . .'

Biddy starts to stand up, so as not to
waste time.

'. . . Lionel Winterbottom,' says Miss Hopeful.

'**What?**' says Biddy. She flops back down.

Lionel is never good, never! I watch as Lionel gets up and walks behind all the other kids in his row. He is pushing their heads as he goes past.

Hey! He just pushed Biddy's head and nearly knocked me over. See? That's what he's like. How can Miss Hopeful give him a prize?

Biddy's shoulders slump. I can feel the sadness oozing out of her. Oh, I hate that Lionel Winterbottom! Look at him, standing up there, pretending to be so good, when he is just the meanest, horriblest, greediest, nastiest human child in the whole entire world! I wish I could pinch him on his cold winterbottom. Or bite him! But I'd get yucky germs and die of food poisoning. So I just sit in Biddy's hair and think **nasty** thoughts about him instead.

Chapter seven

Can you train a goldfish?

As we're walking back to class, Biddy takes Miss Hopeful's hand and politely asks, 'Why did you give Lionel the prize, Miss Hopeful, when he is the **naughtiest** kid in the whole class?'

'Well, Biddy,' Miss Hopeful says, 'I gave the prize to Lionel because he has tried hard to be good this week.'

'But I *have* been good this week,' says Biddy.

'Yes, darling, I know,' Miss Hopeful says. 'But you try to be good every day. I gave Lionel the prize to encourage him to try to be good more often.'

For the rest of the day, me and Biddy can't stop thinking about the book prize.

Lionel probably doesn't even like books! Even if he does, he'll only like books about trucks or trains. I'm wondering if you have to be really **naughty** first, and then be good afterwards to get a 'best behaved' book prize. I bet that is it.

I sit on Biddy's head and try really hard to think of something naughty we could do in class, so that Miss Hopeful will notice when we're good again afterwards. Suddenly, Biddy interrupts me.

'Rolly Polly is just like Lionel,' she whispers to herself.

'Yes,' I say. 'Didn't I say that Rolly Polly is boring and dumb?'

'He doesn't do what he is told,' Biddy whispers again. 'I could teach Rolly Polly to stand on his tail by giving him a prize.' Biddy frowns. 'But what prize could you give to a fish? Fish can't read, so it's no use giving them a book prize.'

'Food!' I yell. 'All that silly goldfish cares about is food.'

Then she thinks of it all by herself. 'Food!' she says. 'That's how they teach dolphins. I'll give him a prize of food.'

Later that afternoon, when me and Biddy get home from school, Biddy runs straight to the kitchen. Then she takes a pinch of fish food out of its container, and holds it right on the surface of the water in the fish tank, above Rolly Polly.

'Come on, don't you want some food?' she says, to encourage him.

Rolly Polly lifts his head out of the water and snatches the food.

WOW! I think. Maybe he isn't as silly as he looks.

'That's it. That's it,' Biddy says, in her best teacher-voice. 'You can do it. That's the way. Nearly there.'

This time, Rolly Polly pushes himself a bit further out of the water and gulps the pinch of food from Biddy's fingertips.

'Yes! You're **very** clever. Good boy,' Biddy tells him. She takes another pinch of food and holds it over the water, a little bit higher than before.

This is such fun! I love it.

And Rolly Polly loves it, too. He stands on his tail, and wiggles and flaps till he jumps up and . . . misses the food.

'Never mind, good try,' Biddy tells Rolly Polly, and holds the next pinch of food lower, so it is easier for him to reach.

Rolly Polly comes out of the water and gulps the food. He is standing right up on his tail.

Then he does it again.

And again.

'Rolly Polly, the famous tricky-dolphin goldfish!' Biddy smiles. She is feeling proud of herself for being such a good teacher.

And she is proud of Rolly Polly, too, for being such a quick learner.

Really, Biddy should be proud of me, because it was **my** idea to give Rolly Polly a prize of food.

Chapter eight
a terrible accident

Rolly Polly loves doing tricks. I love it, too. It is much more interesting than watching him going around and around his goldfish bowl, **gulp-gulp-gulping**. Rolly Polly loves tricks so much that he stands on his tail and gulps food over and over. Until he is so full, the flakes of fish food pop out of his mouth again. He has to chase them around and gulp them again and again and again, before they finally go down.

But he still keeps coming up for more, until he can't stand on his tail and falls over sideways.

'You're exhausted, Rolly Polly,' Biddy tells him. 'Let's take a rest.'

'What? Boring, Rolly Polly,' I tell him. 'Keep going! You don't need a rest!'

Rolly Polly doesn't want to take a boring old rest either. He pops his head up and stands on his tail.

'Okay, but just once more,' Biddy says. Rolly Polly jumps and gulps, and jumps and gulps again, until finally he takes a great big **gulp**, and flops over onto his back.

'Rolly Polly! What's the matter?' Biddy asks him.

'Rolly Polly, don't be lazy,' I say.

But Rolly Polly doesn't reply. He just lies on his side, with his eyes open wide. His mouth opens and closes, and fish food wafts in and out of it.

'Rolly Polly, are you all right?' Biddy says. She picks him up, out of the water. 'Have you got a bellyache?' she asks, and rubs his belly, like Mum does with Matilda. Then she puts him back in the bowl and he floats on his side, flap-flapping and going **backwards**!

'Rolly Polly!' Biddy yells, and lifts him up again and blows air into his mouth to keep him alive, like the ambulance people do on TV when someone is very sick.

Rolly Polly jerks and wiggles as if he is getting better, but when Biddy puts him back in the water, he floats sideways again.

'Mum!' Biddy screams. 'Mum! Rolly Polly's dying.'

'Brigid Lucy!' Mum says when she sees Rolly Polly on his side. 'What have you done?'

'I didn't do anything,' Biddy says. 'He's just sick and dying all by himself.'

I duck into one of Biddy's plaits. I don't want to look at Rolly Polly being all sideways and dead.

'Get Matilda,' Mum tells Biddy. Then she grabs the goldfish bowl. 'Hurry, we have to take Rolly Polly to the vet's,' she says.

'Matilda!' Biddy yells. She runs through the house, with me flapping inside her plait.

'It's an **emergency**,' Biddy tells Matilda when she finds her. 'You have to be good, or Rolly Polly will die.'

'Okay, Biddy,' Matilda says. And she helps Biddy to find her shoes, and runs out to the car with Biddy without whingeing or crying once.

Mum puts Matilda and baby Ellen in their car seats. Me and Biddy sit in the middle with our seatbelt on.

Biddy holds Rolly Polly's bowl carefully on her lap. Rolly Polly is still floating sideways in the bowl. We rush through the traffic to the vet's pet hospital.

All the way, Matilda is being good. She doesn't say a word. When we get out of the car, me and Biddy are good, too. Mum carries Rolly Polly and baby Ellen, and we hold Matilda's hand going across the vet's car park, to make sure she doesn't get run-over-and-squashed-flat-out-dead by a car.

The vet's has got **magic** doors that open all by themselves as soon as they see you. So we rush straight in.

Mum shows Rolly Polly to the nurse sitting behind the counter just inside the door. 'My little girl's goldfish is very sick,' she says.

The nurse looks at Rolly Polly and frowns. 'Oh dear,' she says. 'I'm not sure we can fix goldfish.'

'He's going to die, isn't he?' Biddy asks the nurse. Her voice **crackles** with tears.

'No, he will be okay,' the nurse tells Biddy. 'I'll take him into the vet right now.' She quickly carries Rolly Polly through a swinging doorway and disappears.

Chapter nine
the vet's pet hospital

Wow! I've never been in a vet's pet hospital before. It is just like a pet shop. There are millions of animals in the waiting room. Of course me and Biddy are still worried about Rolly Polly being sick. But we can't help but notice the cockatoos and budgies in cages. And we can't help but smile at all the dogs and mice and rabbits that are being held by their owners. And . . .

Yukki-poo-la-drop-kick! There is a huge evil cream-and-brown Siamese cat sitting on a lady's lap! It's not even in a cage.

'Biddy, don't go near it,' I say. 'Look, it has scary blue see-through eyes, and a red collar with deadly sharp diamonds in it.'

But Biddy does not listen to me. She goes straight up to the cat.

'Hello,' she says to it.

Mum puts baby Ellen and Matilda in the little kids' playpen in the corner of the waiting room. 'Brigid,' she calls, 'come and play with Matilda and Ellen. I have to go and talk to the vet about Rolly Polly.'

'Yes, Mum,' Biddy says, and starts walking toward the playpen.

Whew!

But as soon as Mum disappears into the vet's office, Biddy turns around and runs straight back to the cat!

I dive inside one of Biddy's plaits, and peek out through the smallest hole in **infinity**. Biddy is touching the cat's head. It closes its eyes and curves its body until it slides right under Biddy's hand.

'His name is Zhmiggie,' the cat-owner lady says.

'Biddy, please,' I say. My voice is trembling. 'Let's go. Cats love to catch little creatures. Even if they are invisible.'

'He likes you,' the cat-owner lady tells Biddy. 'Would you like to hold him for a minute while I go to the toilet?'

'What?' I say. 'No! Biddy, please. We have to go and look after Matilda and Ellen.' I'm begging her.

But Biddy says, 'Yes, please,' to the cat-owner lady. And then she sits in a chair, with the cat on her lap. She is smiling, and pretending the cat is her very own pet.

Just then, the vet's magic door opens, and in comes a lady with a massive hungry guard dog and a boy . . .

The boy is Lionel Winterbottom.

'Lionel Winterbottom?' Biddy whispers to herself. 'He's got a dog! How can he have a dog and a book prize?' She turns her face away, so she doesn't have to see him.

Then, **Oo-laa-coo-laa-stinky-pooh-laa!** Lionel turns around and sees me and Biddy. He starts to smirk. It is a very mean smirk.

'Biddy! Biddy!' I yell. 'Lionel is going to do something horrible to us. Biddy, look! He's pulling on the dog's lead.'

'Let me hold Bruiser, Mum,' Lionel is saying.

'No, darling, he is too strong for you,' Mrs Winterbottom tells him.

'I said, let me hold him,' Lionel yells in a rude voice. 'Give me the lead!' he shouts and snatches the lead away from his mother.

'Lionel. **Shhh!**' his mother whispers. 'Okay, you can have the lead, but hold it tight. And stay right here.'

But Lionel doesn't stay right there. He starts walking straight towards me and Biddy. He **ignores** his mother, who is yelling, 'Lionel! Lionel! Where are you going? Bring Bruiser back here right now, please.'

As soon as Zhmiggie the cat sees Lionel's huge, hungry dog looking at him, he doesn't want Biddy to stroke him any more. He stands up tall on Biddy's lap, hissing and arching his back, and showing all his terrifying razor-sharp teeth. My body shivers with fright and I snuggle down further into Biddy's plait.

Lionel stops right in front of us. 'My dog likes cats,' he says. 'Would you like to eat this cat, Bruiser?' He brings his dog closer to Zhmiggie.

'Cats are stupid, hey, Bruiser?' Lionel says to the dog. 'It was a cat's fault Bruiser got hit by a car,' Lionel adds.

'Well, that's your dog's own fault for chasing cats,' Biddy says. 'Anyway, he can't have got run over. I've seen a properly run-over dog and it was squashed flat. You're a big fat liar!'

'I am not!' Lionel says.

'You are so!' says Biddy.

'Am not,' Lionel says, more loudly. He lifts up his hand.

He's going to hit Biddy! 'Get away, Lionel,' I scream, jumping out of Biddy's plait. 'I will scratch you and bite you to death if you touch my friend, Biddy.'

Then . . .

'**Hissss!**' Zhmiggie the cat snarls. He lashes out with his deadly sharp claws and . . .

'**Raaahhoow!**' Zhmiggie scratches Lionel's hand to bits.

'**Ahhh!**' Lionel screams. He shows the red scratch-marks on his hand to everyone in the waiting room. 'Her cat attacked me!'

Wow! Did you see that? Zhmiggie is a guard cat.

'Go, Zhmiggie, go,' I yell. 'Scratch Lionel. Bite him.' I run across Biddy's head and jump up and down on top of her ear.

'You're dead,' Lionel says to Biddy. His face is twisted up with wildness. 'Kill, Bruiser!' he yells to the dog, and points at us.

'**Whooff!**' Bruiser says, and jumps towards Biddy.

Before I can even think of a way to save Biddy, Zhmiggie the cat leaps into the air and lands on Bruiser's back with his claws out. '**Raaahhoow!**' Zhmiggie growls, as he scratches and bites.

'**Orr, orr, orr!**' Bruiser screams and jumps back.

Smack! Bruiser knocks Lionel into a man with a huge green parrot on his shoulder.

'**Craaakkk!**' the parrot screams. Then it bites Lionel on the ear.

Me and Biddy crack up laughing.

Lionel runs in circles, screaming and flapping his arms. He is trying to get the parrot to let go of his ear. Bruiser spins around in circles as well, trying to get Zhmiggie off his back.

Lionel's mum runs after them saying, 'Lionel, darling. Oh, Lionel, my poor dear!' And, 'Bruiser!' And, 'Bruiser, sit!'

Chapter ten

The end—
nearly

Mum and the vet come racing out of
the vet's office to see what all the noise
is about. The vet grabs Zhmiggie from
Bruiser's back with his huge hairy hands
and holds the cat tight, to stop him from
scratching.

'Get that dog under control,' the vet tells
Lionel's mum.

'Stand still, young man,' he tells Lionel.
And he pats and talks to the parrot until it
lets go of Lionel's ear. As soon as the parrot
does let go, the vet says, 'Into my office so I
can see about that ear.'

And takes them into his office! Which
is **totally** not fair because it wasn't even
their turn.

Biddy says, 'Goodbye, Lionel. Have a nice day.'

But Lionel doesn't hear her because he is holding his ear and cuddling his mum and crying like a little baby **sooky** boy.

Me and Biddy can't help but giggle.

Mum says, 'Brigid Lucy. I hope you didn't have anything to do with that kerfuffle.'

'Is Rolly Polly all right?' Biddy asks, to stop Mum from asking questions about the cat-Lionel-dog fight.

'Yes, he's fine,' Mum says. Then she pauses in a making-up-a-story kind-of way and quickly adds, 'But he has to stay in hospital for a few hours, so Dad will pick him up on his way home from work.'

Is Mum **fibbing**? She definitely has a kind of telling-fibs look in her eyes. But I can't study her properly, because she turns away and picks up baby Ellen and Matilda from the playpen.

Matilda has had enough of being good now that the emergency is over, so she

starts crying, 'Leeb me! Leeb me! Don'
wanna go! Wanna play.'

She cries all the way home from
the vet's.

Mum says it is because Matilda is
exhausted. So Mum goes and lies down
with Matilda and baby Ellen to have
a rest.

Me and Biddy sit on the couch, waiting for
Dad to pick up Rolly Polly and bring him
home.

Wasn't the trip to the vet's the best
fun ever? I just loved the bit when Lionel
got scratched by the cat, and his ear got
bitten by the parrot. Biddy loved it, too.
She would like to run over to next door and
tell our neighbour, Jamie, all about it. But
we don't, because you're not allowed to
be happy when your pet goldfish is ill in
hospital. So Biddy sits by the window, and
sucks her thumb instead.

I am so happy about the fun we have just had, I don't even care if Biddy is being bestest friends with her thumb. I just cuddle up in my nest of hair behind Biddy's neck, and play the 'memory video' of Lionel and his dog at the vet's, over and over in my mind.

When we hear Dad's car pulling up outside the house, we run out to meet him.

'Dad, is **Rolly Polly** okay?' Biddy asks. She opens the car door and lifts the goldfish bowl from the front seat.

The bowl is empty.

'Where's Rolly Polly?' Biddy says.

'Brigid,' Dad says. He walks quickly around the car. His teeth are all clenched up, and he is trying not to shout. 'Did you overfeed the goldfish?'

Biddy's eyes go wide and she lifts her shoulders in a depends-what-you-mean-by-overfeed kind-of way.

'The vet said he was nearly **bursting** with food,' Dad yells.

'Is he dead, Daddy?' Biddy says. Her voice is cracking with sadness.

'No, Rolly Polly is not dead,' Mum shouts from the steps. She is glaring at Dad.

'Then where is he?' Biddy asks.

'He's . . .' Dad says, thinking really hard.

But before he can say anything, Mum says, 'Rolly Polly has . . . gone to live in Mrs Greenaway's pond down the street, so he can be with all the other goldfish.'

She's doing it again. She has that funny making-up-stories look on her face. I wonder if she is really telling fibs.

But Biddy doesn't even notice Mum's fibbing-face. She just says, 'Oh. Is Rolly Polly missing me?'

'You can go and visit him,' Mum tells Biddy. 'But you are **not** allowed to give him too much food!'

'No, Mum, I won't,' Biddy says. Her face is serious. 'I won't even feed him at all.'

So Rolly Polly went to live in Mrs Greenaway's pond. But when me and Biddy go and visit, we can't find him. We sit beside the pond and call, 'Rolly Polly, Rolly Polly.'

But guess what? Nine hundred and ten goldfish come up to the surface, but none of them looks like Rolly Polly.

'Perhaps Rolly has changed after being so **sick**,' Biddy says. 'How will I know which one he is?'

Then—and I didn't suggest it at all— Biddy decides all by herself to try holding a little bit of food above the water, to see which fish is Rolly Polly. Which is not feeding the fish, exactly, it is just doing a test.

Biddy takes just a tiny pinch of flakes from Mrs Greenaway's special fish food.

She holds it above the water. Quick as a flash, a goldfish stands on his tail and gulps down the food.

'Rolly Polly!' Biddy laughs. 'It's you. My Rolly Polly.'

'That's not Rolly Polly,' I say. 'That one has a white spot on his face. Rolly Polly didn't have a white spot.'

But Biddy doesn't listen to me. She takes another pinch of food out of the tin and holds it above the water. 'Come on, Rolly Polly,' she says.

And up comes a fish with a black tip on his fin. Then, one with googly eyes. Then, one with a fluffy **floppy** tail. Until there are so many different-shaped goldfish standing on their tails to gobble food from Biddy's fingertips that I can't remember what the old Rolly Polly looked like.

And Biddy doesn't care whether the fish with black fins or googly eyes or a frilly tail is the old Rolly Polly. She just reckons that, when she holds up a pinch of food,

and a fish pops out its head to take the food, then that fish is Rolly Polly.

But don't worry. Biddy never overfeeds any of the fish. There are so many fish in Mrs Greenaway's pond that by the time she has given a pinch of food to each of them, we are both ready to play another game.

So we all live **happily ever after**.

Epilogue

Except that we can't play with Rolly Polly at Mrs Greenaway's place every day. But that doesn't matter because guess what? Biddy's mum takes us to City Library, which is like a whole three-storey building full of books—millions and **trillions** of books all on top of each other, right up to the ceiling. And the library lady lets us borrow them. Six at a time!

I totally love it when Biddy's mum reads us the stories about goblins and witches and dragons, and magic, and princes, and princesses getting married in glass slippers, and scary stepmothers and faraway lands where animals can talk to humans—and humans listen!

But I love it more when me and Biddy actually get to go inside a magical story—I mean in real life, not in the book. It is true. It . . .

Ooops! I shouldn't have told you about that.

No, it's nothing. Well . . .

No, really. I can't tell you about it because I'm too busy to talk. And anyway we've run out of pages, so I will just have to tell you in another book.

Bye!

Magical creatures

Slivigools—danger rating—tremendously acutely high

Slivigools are extremely beautiful and fun-loving beings. They have special nostrils that allow them to breathe underwater and in the air. They love to study their reflections in the water, to comb their long hair, and to play among the pink, waving roots of paperbark trees. But they are very private and hate anyone looking at them. If you stare at them they will scream an ear-piercing scream until they knock you out, and then they will wrap their hair around your legs and drown you to death.

Fillikizard dragons—danger rating—tremendously acutely high

Fillikizard dragons are small crocodile-like creatures, that have a frill of armour around their necks. They are very powerful hunters. Their back legs spin around like wheels, so they can run terribly fast. They have such huge mouths, they can eat other creatures twice their size. Never try to capture a fillikizard dragon, because they can kill you dead with a blast of their foul breaths from three metres away. If you are too big for them to swallow up, they will slobber all over you and you will stink forever.

Choolkas—danger rating—high

Choolkas live in the highest branches of the tallest trees and only come out late at night. They look cute and gentle and kind, with their big blue eyes, and their hairy-grandfather kind-of faces. But, beneath their soft grey fur, they have the most vicious pointy cat-like teeth, and sharp-as-a-dagger claws. Never go walking without a torch at night, or you will get choolka-gashes all over your knees and elbows.

Yebil yebils —danger rating—a bit high

Yebils yebils are mischievous little creatures that love to see children get hurt. They own every piece of earth in the whole wide world. They demand that everyone ask permission to walk anywhere. If you don't ask permission, they will pretend to be a piece of vine or a rock or a hole in the footpath and trip you over. Then they bend over laughing and squealing with delight. Make sure you always call out, 'Please can I play on this earth?' before you go walking in a new place.

Ympes—Danger rating—low

These tiny creatures can join themselves to, and become part of, other animals and plants. They often glue themselves to a bird's feathers and fly all over the world as part of that bird. They can also melt into a tree and grow there, making the blossom on part of the tree a different colour to the blossom on the rest of the tree. They also climb into a horse's ears and take control of the horse, so it runs around the paddock, kicking and bucking and bolting, for no reason. Always check your horse's ears for ympes before you go for a ride.

Magical swearwords

Yucki-toenails!
Yukki-poo-la-drop-kick!
Oo-laa-coo-laa-stinky-pooh-laa!

Magical unlocking-spell words

Oo-pen-doe-nous!
Till-gäng-lig!

Look out for …

Brigid Lucy
and the Princess Tower

Biddy is excited when she spots a real-life
Princess Tower from the window of the
train. So is the invisible imp that lives in
Biddy's hair.

Mum says the tower is a cathedral, but
what do grown-ups know?

When Biddy and the imp investigate
further, they discover that Princess
Rapunzel is trapped inside the tower.

Can Biddy save the day?

Acknowledgements

To the Tasmanian Writer's Centre, for giving me a residency in their wonderful Hobart studio, where trying to blend in with this old world and beautiful city, my little imp got me into lots of delicious trouble. To Libby and Margrete, for generously inviting me to join their table, which lead to our friendship and working relationship. And, most importantly, to my niece, Brigid Tony Izod, who inspired the character Brigid Lucy.